Eloise Wilkin's
Mother Goose

A GOLDEN BOOK • NEW YORK
Western Publishing Company, Inc.
Racine, Wisconsin 53404

Baa, Baa, Black Sheep

Baa, baa, black sheep, have you any wool?
Yes, sir, yes, sir, three bags full.
One for my master, one for my dame,
And one for the little boy
Who lives in the lane.

Old King Cole

Old King Cole was a merry old soul,
And a merry old soul was he.
He called for his pipe,
He called for his bowl,
And he called for his fiddlers three!

Little Jack Horner

Little Jack Horner sat in a corner,
Eating his Christmas pie.
He put in his thumb and pulled out a plum,
And said, "What a good boy am I!"

Little Miss Muffet

Little Miss Muffet sat on a tuffet,
Eating her curds and whey.
There came a big spider,
And sat down beside her,
And frightened Miss Muffet away.

Sing a Song of Sixpence

Sing a song of sixpence,
A pocket full of rye,
Four-and-twenty blackbirds
Baked in a pie!
When the pie was opened
The birds began to sing.
Wasn't that a dainty dish
To set before the King?

Little Girls

What are little girls
    made of,
    made of?
What are little girls
    made of?
Sugar and spice
And everything nice.
That's what little girls
    are made of.

Little Boys

What are little boys
   made of,
   made of?
What are little boys
   made of?
Snakes and snails
And puppy-dogs' tails.
That's what little boys
   are made of.

Pease Porridge

Pease porridge hot,
Pease porridge cold,
Pease porridge in the pot,
Nine days old.

The Old Woman

There was an old woman
Who lived in a shoe.
She had so many children
She didn't know what to do.
She gave them some broth,
Without any bread,
Then spanked them all soundly,
And sent them to bed.

Little Polly Flinders

Little Polly Flinders
Sat among the cinders,
Warming her pretty toes!
Her mother came and caught her,
And spanked her little daughter,
For spoiling her nice new clothes.

A Dillar, A Dollar

A dillar, a dollar,
A ten o'clock scholar,
What makes you come so soon?
You used to come at ten o'clock,
And now you come at noon.

Ride a Cockhorse

Ride a cockhorse to Banbury Cross,
To see a fine lady upon a white horse.
Rings on her fingers,
And bells on her toes,
She shall have music
Wherever she goes.

Tom, Tom, the Piper's Son

Tom, Tom, the Piper's son
Stole a pig, and away he run.
The pig was eat,
And Tom was beat,
And Tom went crying
Down the street.

Jack and Jill

Jack and Jill went up the hill
To fetch a pail of water.
Jack fell down and broke his crown,
And Jill came tumbling after.

Georgie Porgie

Georgie Porgie, pudding and pie,
Kissed the girls and made them cry.
When the boys came out to play,
Georgie Porgie ran away.

Pussycat, Pussycat

"Pussycat, pussycat, where have you been?"
"I've been to London to visit the Queen."
"Pussycat, pussycat, what did you there?"
"I frightened a little mouse under her chair."

Peter, Peter, Pumpkin Eater

Peter, Peter, pumpkin eater,
Had a wife and couldn't keep her.
He put her in a pumpkin shell,
And there he kept her very well.

Old Mother Hubbard

Old Mother Hubbard
Went to the cupboard
To get her poor dog a bone.
But when she got there,
The cupboard was bare,
And so the poor dog had none.

Little Boy Blue

Little Boy Blue,
Come blow your horn!
The sheep's in the meadow,
The cow's in the corn.
Where is the boy
Who looks after the sheep?
He's under the haystack,
Fast asleep!

Little Bo-Peep

Little Bo-Peep has lost her sheep,
And can't tell where to find them.
Leave them alone
And they'll come home,
Wagging their tails behind them.

Pat-a-Cake, Pat-a-Cake

Pat-a-cake, pat-a-cake, baker's man!
Bake me a cake as fast as you can.
Roll it and pat it
And mark it with "B"
And put it in the oven
For baby and me.

Mary Had a Little Lamb

Mary had a little lamb,
Its fleece was white as snow.
And everywhere that Mary went
The lamb was sure to go.